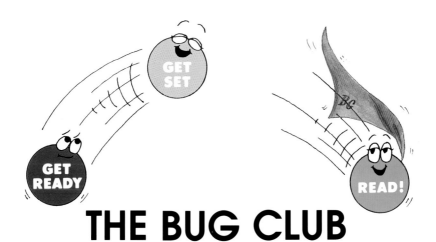

THE BUG CLUB

All inquiries should be addressed to:
Barron's Educational Series, Inc.
250 Wireless Boulevard
Hauppauge, NY 11788

International Standard Book Number 0-8120-4730-3

Library of Congress Catalog Card Number 91-565

Library of Congress Cataloging-in-Publication Data

Erickson, Gina Clegg.
    The bug club / Gina Clegg Erickson and Kelli C. Foster :
illustrations by Kerri Gifford.
        p. cm.—(Get ready...get set...read!)
Summary: A bug named Pug goes off to investigate a jug.
    ISBN: 0-8120-4730-3
    (1. Insects—Fiction   2. Stories in rhyme.)
I. Foster, Kelli C.   II. Gifford, Kerri, ill. III. Title. IV. Series: Erickson,
Gina Clegg. Get ready...get set...read!
PZ8.3.E787Bu   1991
(E)—dc20   91-565
                                           CIP
                                         AC

PRINTED IN HONG KONG

4   9927   987

GET READY...GET SET...READ!

THE BUG CLUB

by
Foster & Erickson

Illustrations by
Kerri Gifford

BARRON'S

The bug club met

on the old red rug.

Look up there.
What is in the jug?

"Let's find out,"
said Pug the bug.

Away ran Pug . . .
off the rug,

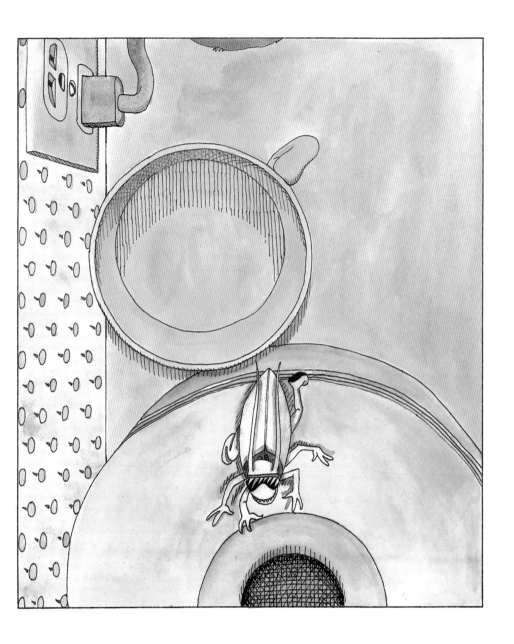

on the plug,
to the mug,
and up, up the jug.

There is Pug
at the top of the jug.

Pug, what is in the jug?

Down, down went Pug
into the jug.

What is in the jug?
Pug is in the jug!

"Let's help Pug!"
said the bugs.
Away they ran off the rug,

on the plug,
to the mug,
and up, up the jug.

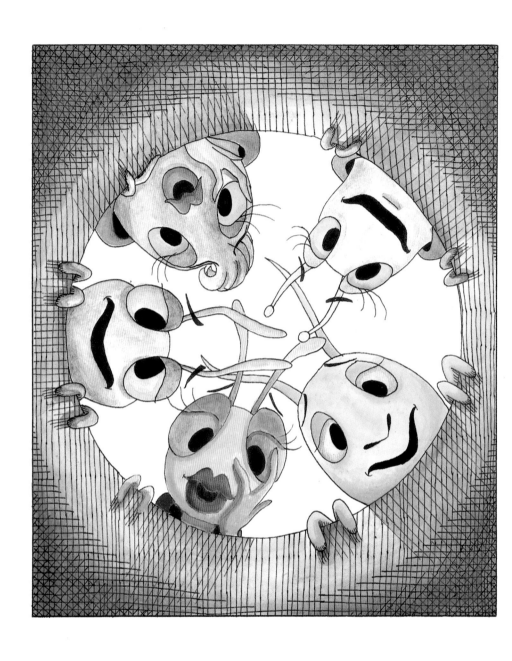

Pug?

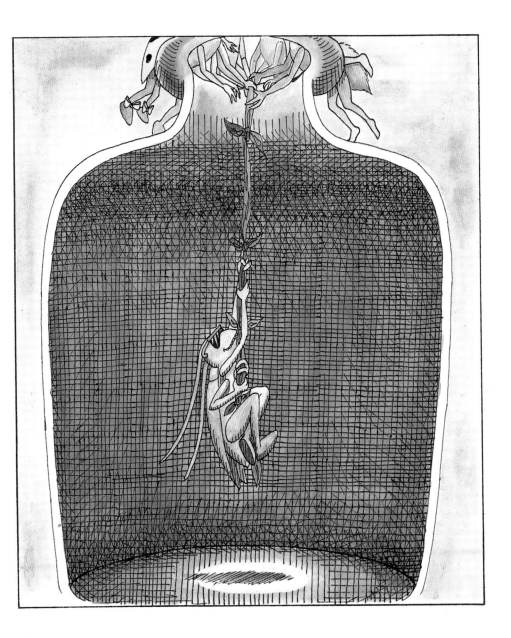

With a tug
and a chug
up, up came Pug.

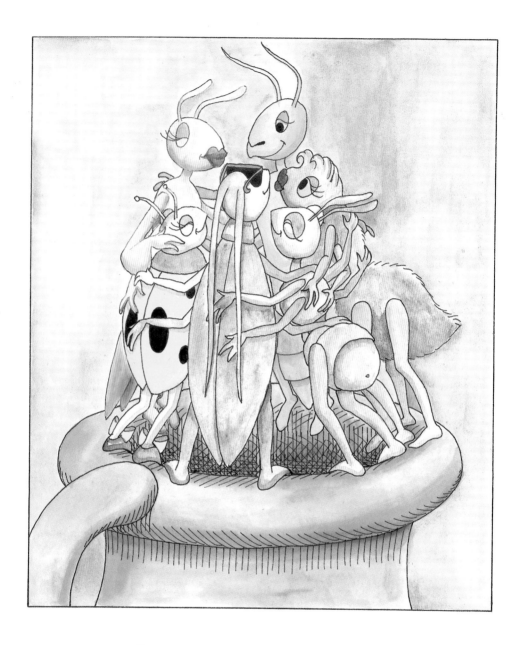

On top of the jug
the bug club hugs.

The End

The UG Word Family

bug
bugs
rug
jug
Pug
mug
tug
hugs
plug
chug

Sight Words

a
of
to
old
out
the
away
down
into
look
said
they
what
there

Dear Parents and Educators:

Welcome to *Get Ready...Get Set...Read!*

We've created these books to introduce children to the magic of reading.

Each story in the series is built around one or two word families. For example, *A Mop for Pop* uses the OP word family. Letters and letter blends are added to OP to form words such as TOP, LOP, and STOP. As you can see, once children are able to read OP, it is a simple task for them to read the entire word family. In addition to word families, we have used a limited number of "sight words." These are words found to occur with high frequency in the books your child will soon be reading. Being able to identify sight words greatly increases reading skill.

You might find the steps outlined on the facing page useful in guiding your work with your beginning reader.

We had great fun creating these books, and great pleasure sharing them with our children. We hope *Get Ready...Get Set...Read!* helps make this first step in reading fun for you and your new reader.

Kelli C. Foster, PhD
Educational Psychologist

Gina Clegg Erickson, MA
Reading Specialist

Guidelines for Using *Get Ready...Get Set...Read!*

Step 1.   Read the story to your child.

Step 2.   Have your child read the Word Family list
           aloud several times.

Step 3.   Invent new words for the list. Print each new
           combination for your child to read.
           Remember, nonsense words can be used
           (*dat, kat, gat*).

Step 4.   Read the story *with* your child. He or she reads
           all of the Word Family words; you read the rest.

Step 5.   Have your child read the Sight Word list
           aloud several times.

Step 6.   Read the story *with* your child again. This time
           he or she reads the words from both lists;
           you read the rest.

Step 7.   Your child reads the entire book to you!

Titles in the

Series:

SET 1

Find Nat
The Sled Surprise
Sometimes I Wish
A Mop for Pop
The Bug Club
BRING-IT-ALL-TOGETHER BOOKS
What a Day for Flying!
Bat's Surprise

SET 2

The Tan Can
The Best Pets Yet
Pip and Kip
Frog Knows Best
Bub and Chub
BRING-IT-ALL-TOGETHER BOOKS
Where Is the Treasure?
What a Trip!

SET 3

Jake and the Snake
Jeepers Creepers
Two Fine Swine
What Rose Does Not Know
Pink and Blue
BRING-IT-ALL-TOGETHER BOOKS
The Pancake Day
Hide and Seek

SET 4

Whiptail of Blackshale Trail
Colleen and the Bean
Dwight and the Trilobite
The Old Man at the Moat
By the Light of the Moon
BRING-IT-ALL-TOGETHER BOOKS
Night Light
The Crossing

SET 5

Tall and Small
Bounder's Sound
How to Catch a Butterfly
Ludlow Grows Up
Matthew's Brew
BRING-IT-ALL-TOGETHER BOOKS
Snow in July
Let's Play Ball